READING TO PEANUT

by **Leda Schubert**

illustrated by
Amanda Haley

Holiday House / New York

Text copyright © 2011 by Leda Schubert
Illustrations copyright © 2011 by Amanda Haley
All Rights Reserved
HOLIDAY HOUSE is registered in the U.S. Patent and Trademark Office.
Printed and Bound in April 2011 at Tien Wah Press,
Johor Bahru, Johor, Malaysia.
The text typeface is Providance Sans.
The artwork was created with acrylic, gouache, colored pencils, and pastel pencils.
www.holidayhouse.com
First Edition
1 3 5 7 9 10 8 6 4 2

Library of Congress Cataloging-in-Publication Data
Schubert, Leda.
Reading to Peanut / by Leda Schubert ; illustrated by Amanda Haley. — 1st ed.
p. cm.
Summary: Lucy works hard to learn to read and write before her dog's birthday.
ISBN 978-0-8234-2339-2 (hardcover)
[1. Reading—Fiction. 2. Writing—Fiction. 3. Family life—Fiction. 4. Dogs—Fiction.]
I. Haley, Amanda, ill. II. Title.
PZ7.S38345Re 2011
[E]—dc22
2010031412

Lucy lived with Mom, Dad, and Peanut in a little house with a big yard.

One morning Lucy said, "I need
to learn to read and write."
"Why?" Dad asked.
"I can't tell you yet," said Lucy.

She collected her markers and sticky notes. "Let's make signs, like in school."

Lucy drew a picture on a sticky note, and Dad wrote a word: D-A-D. Lucy pressed the note onto Dad's nose,

but it fell off

and Peanut chewed it.

"Uh-oh," said Lucy.

She drew another picture on a sticky note, and Dad wrote M-O-M. Lucy stuck it on Mom's chin, but the note fell off, and Peanut chewed it.

"Silly dog," Lucy said.
"You're not helping!"
She fed him a biscuit.
"Want to work in the garden?"
Mom asked.
"Sure," said Lucy.

Mom hoed a long row,
and Lucy dropped in seeds.

She drew a
picture, and Mom
wrote *P-E-A-S.*

Next they planted
bean seeds.

Lucy drew another
picture, and Mom
wrote *B-E-A-N-S.*

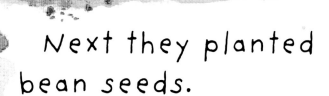

Lucy made up a song.

"Beans and peas, peas and beans, We are planting lots of greens!"

They planted more seeds. Lucy drew a picture, and Mom wrote C-O-R-N. "Thinking about corn makes me hungry," Lucy said, so they hurried inside for lunch.

While they ate, it started to rain. Peanut barked and barked at the front door, so Lucy let him out.

He dug in the muddy garden
and mixed up all the seeds.
"Bad puppy," Lucy said.

"We can plant again later," Mom said.
"First let's do a sign," said Lucy, and
she told Mom what to write.

M-I-X-E-D V-E-G-E-T-A-B-L-E-S.
Lucy drew a picture and sang,
"X and M and L and V
Are letters I have learned to see."

Lucy yawned, and Mom wrote N-A-P.

Lucy read the word to Peanut,
and
Peanut
chewed it.

Then Lucy lay down on her bed, and Peanut climbed up, too. Lucy sang,

"Peanut's climbing on my lap. We will take a little nap!"

Mom read a story, and Lucy and Peanut fell asleep.

When they woke, the sun came out, and Mom and Lucy replanted the vegetables.

Then Dad grilled hamburgers while Mom and Lucy wrote *E-A-T* on a sticky note.

Peanut chewed it, and Lucy laughed. "He's learning to read, too," she said.

For the next few weeks, Lucy, Mom, and Dad made signs; and Lucy read them all to Peanut.

She worked hard copying letters and words.

Finally she was ready, and just in time, too.

She asked Mom to help her
in the kitchen. Together they
cooked beans, corn, carrots, and
peas along with eggs and cheese.

Lucy shaped it all into a cake
and placed it in Peanut's bowl,
but she didn't let him eat it.

Not yet.

She had a bigger surprise
that she had made all by herself:
a birthday card for Peanut.

She read it aloud.
"Happy birthday to you,
I love you, I do.
We all grew some veggies,
And these are for you."

"You did it!" Dad said. "You learned
to read and write, and now I know why!"
"It was important," Lucy said proudly.

She put the card on the shelf
where Peanut couldn't reach it.
He ate his cake instead.

That night Mom wrote
G-O-O-D N-I-G-H-T. Lucy drew
a moon and climbed into bed,
where she made one more sign.

She drew a heart and wrote K-I-S-S.
Mom kissed Lucy, Lucy kissed Mom,
and Peanut kissed everybody.